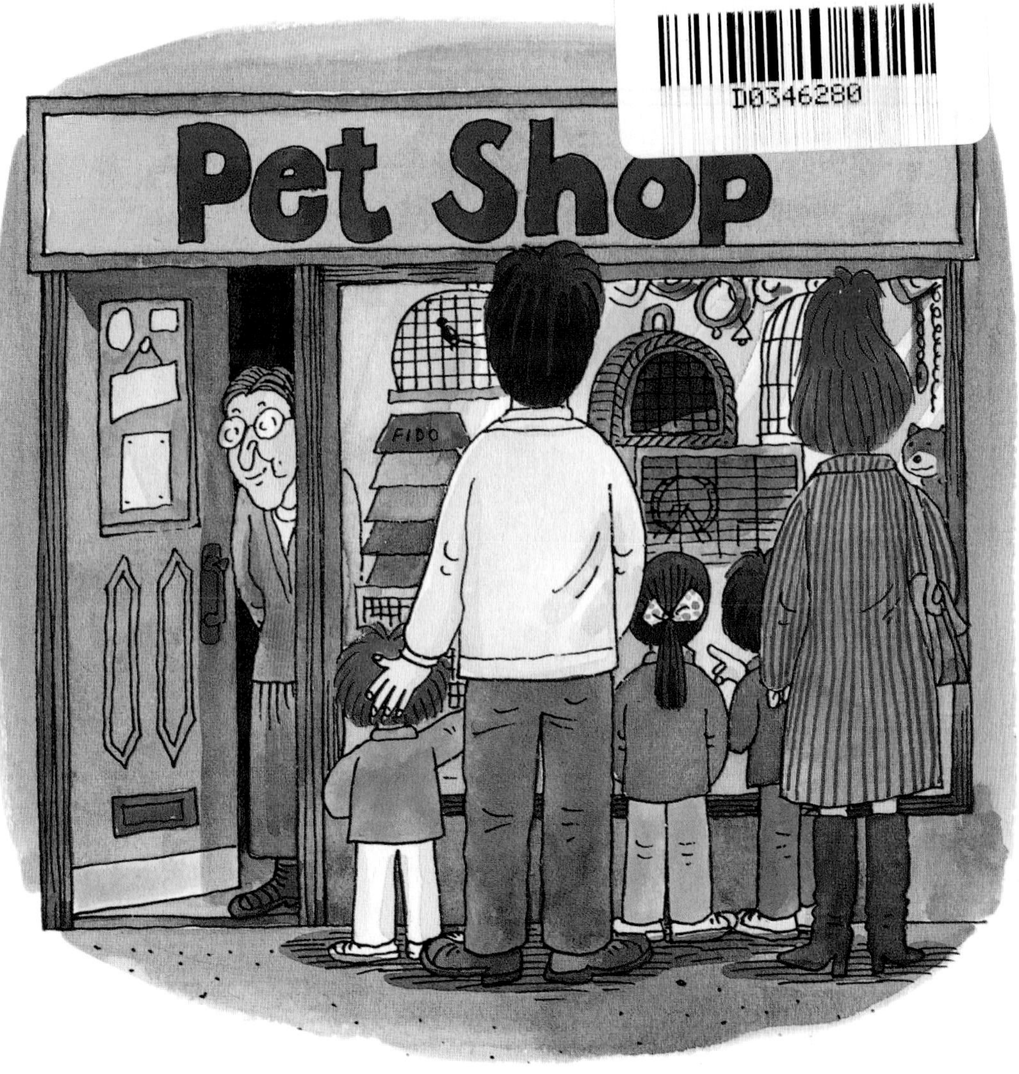

Everyone wanted a pet.

Chip wanted a rat.

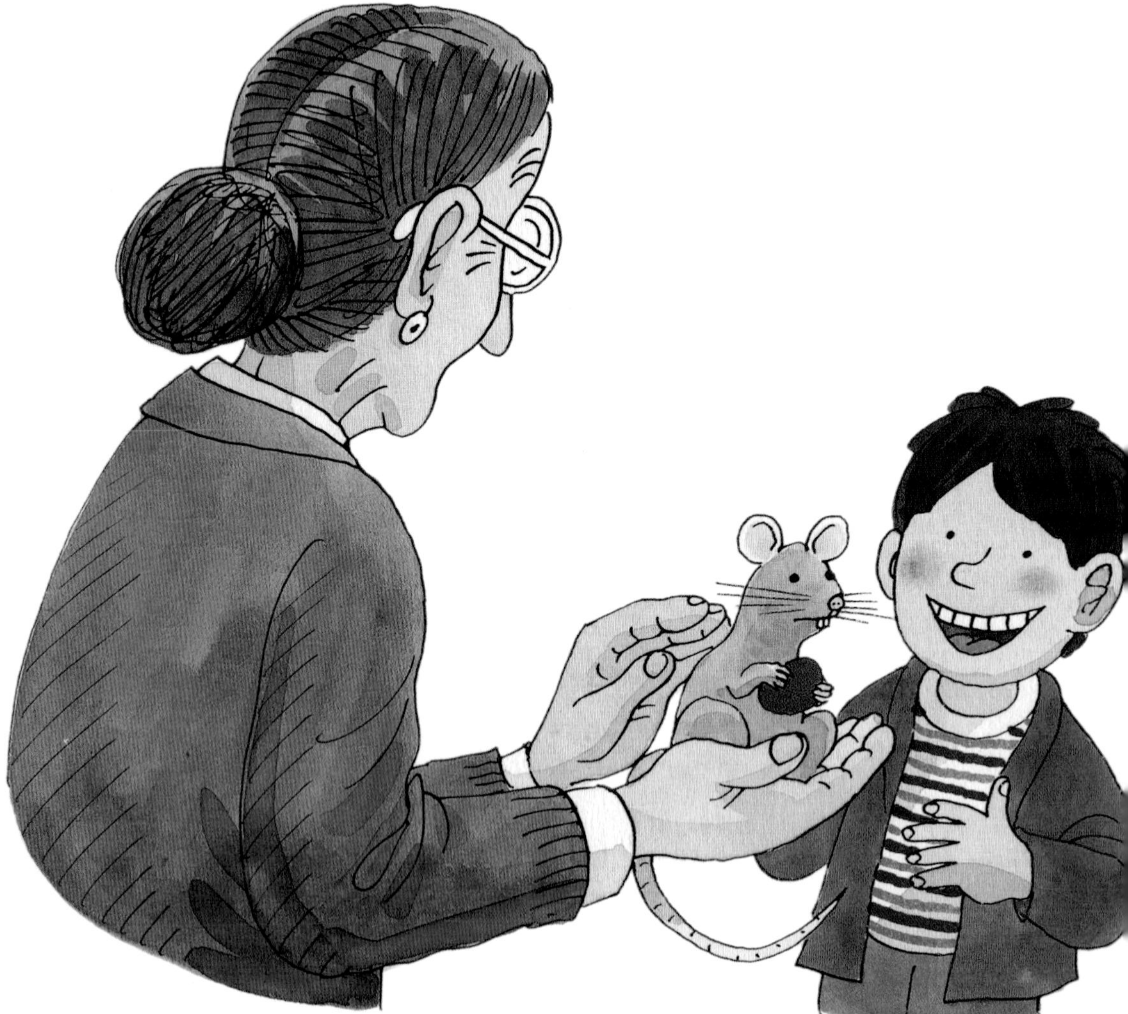

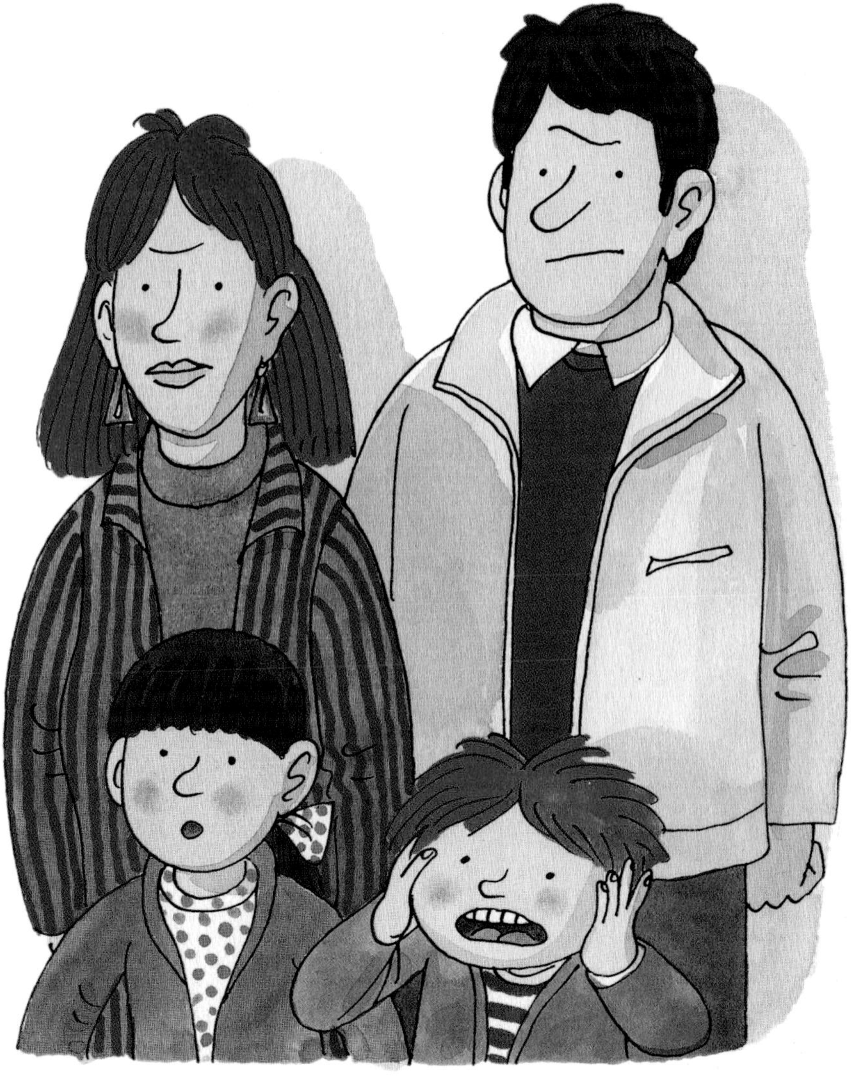

“Oh no!” said everyone.

Biff wanted a spider.

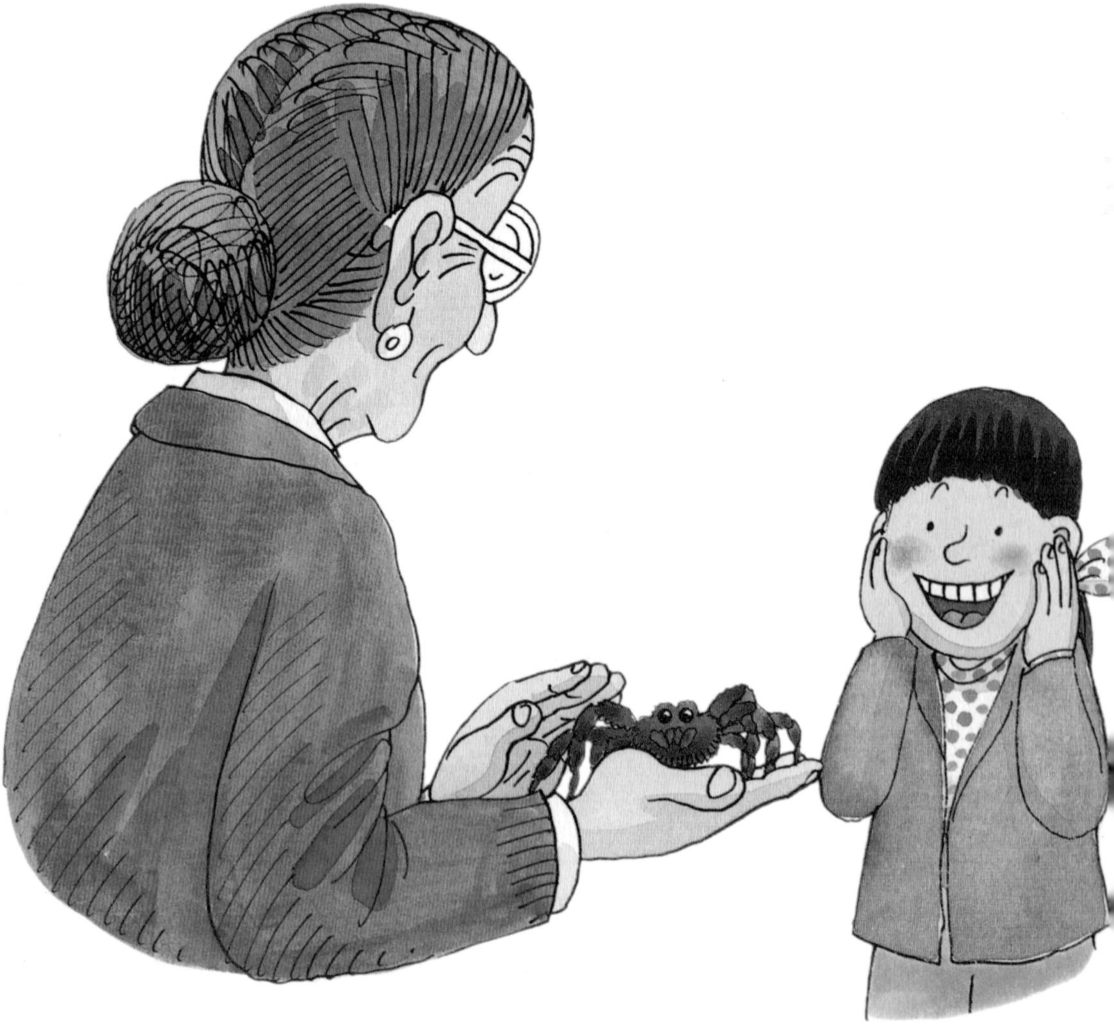

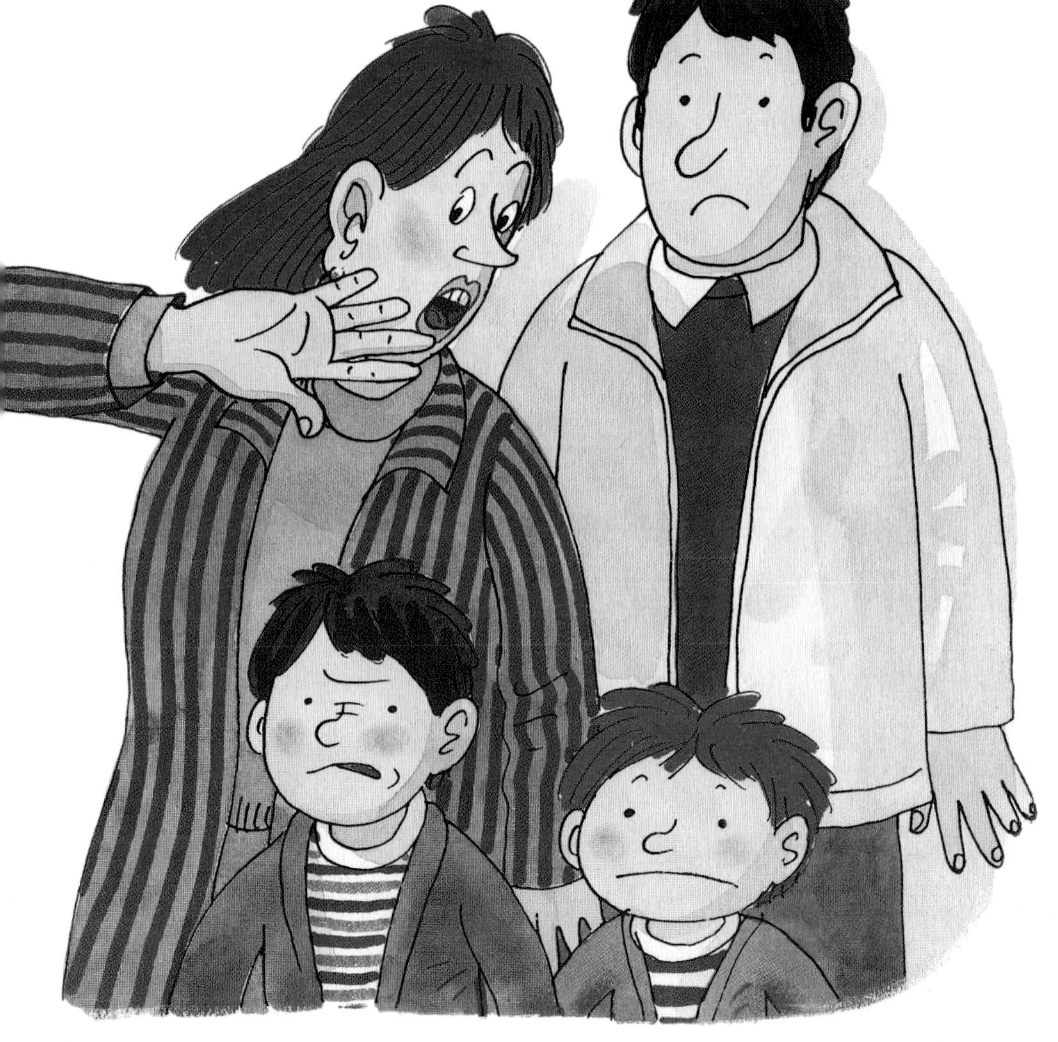

“Oh no!” said everyone.

Kipper wanted a snake.

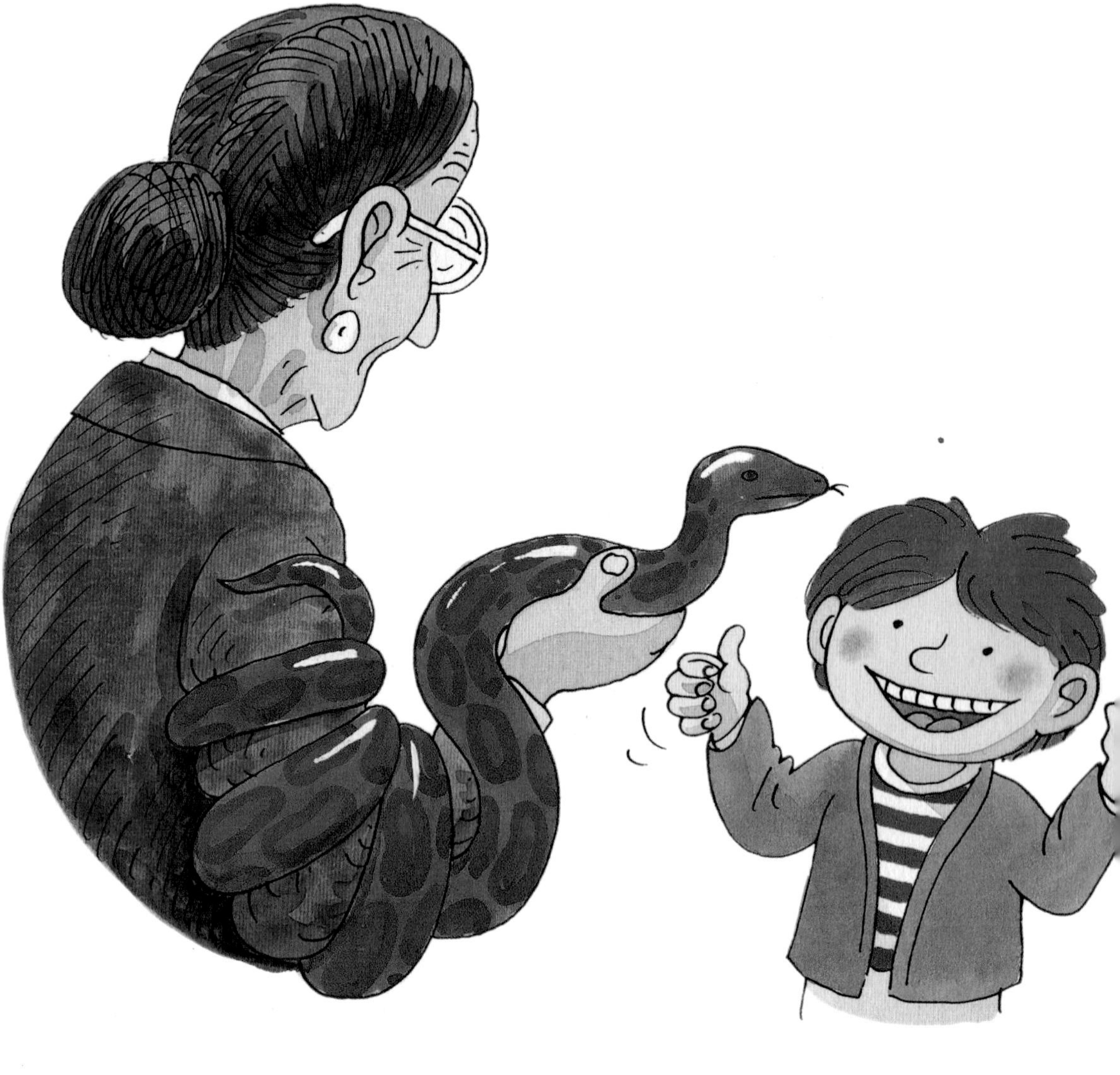

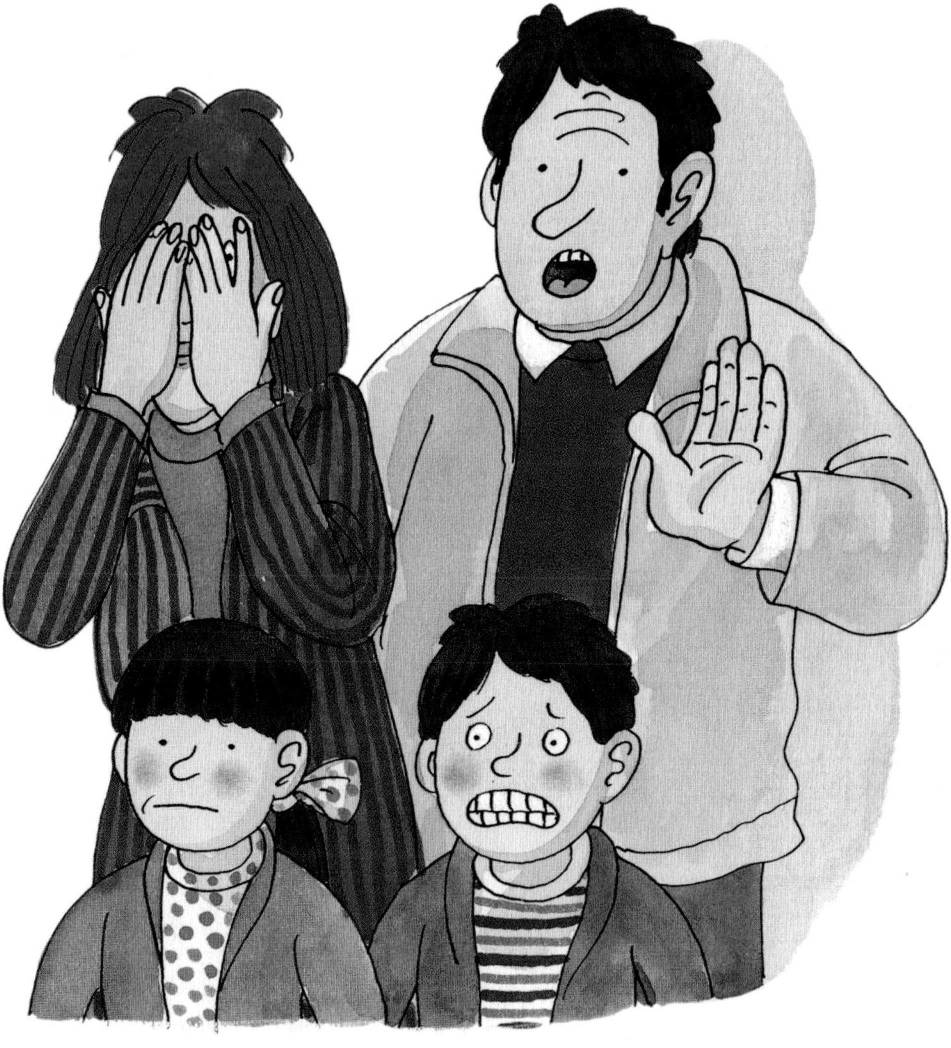

“Oh no!” said everyone.

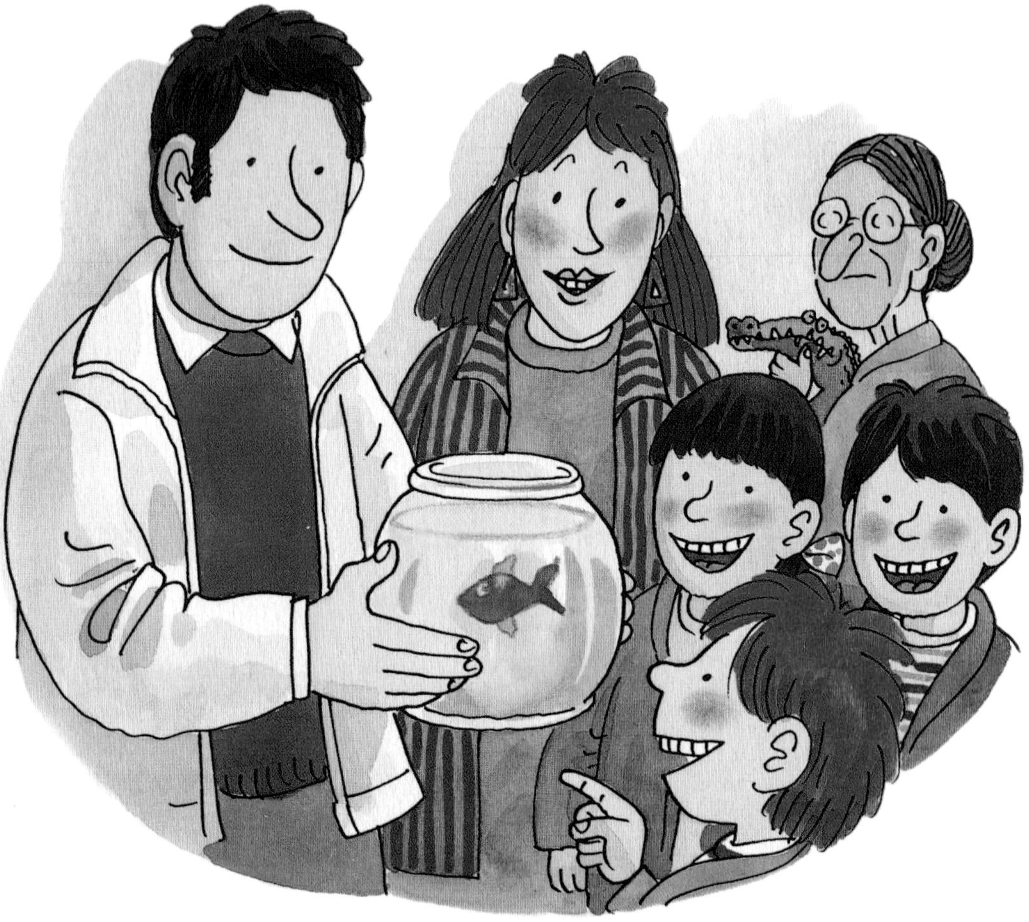

Everyone wanted a goldfish.